The Happy Tale of Two Cats

By Cathy M. Rosenthal

Illustrated by Jessica Warrick

Pet Pundit Publishing • Austin, Texas

Published in the United States of America by Pet Pundit Publishing

First Edition, 2012

ISBN 978-0-9853752-1-8

Library of Congress Control Number: 2012916613

Pet Pundit Publishing
Austin, Texas
info@petpundit.com
www.petpunditpublishing.com

Printed in the United States of America

Until they all find
good homes...

In the very same town, on the very same street,

in two different houses, live two cats.

One cat is happy.

The other cat is unhappy.

The happy cat lives in a home with a family that loves her.

The unhappy cat spends
most of her time alone,
running away from loud voices
and feet that chase her.

The happy cat has a collar and an ID tag with her name "Happy" on it.

No one gives the unhappy cat a collar or an ID tag.

If she gets lost, she may never get home again.

Happy helps her family around the house.

She helps mom read.

She helps dad work.

She helps the children sleep during the night.

She helps them make
their beds in the morning.

Sadly, no one wants the unhappy cat's help around the house.

Happy's family plays
with her every day.
They know she loves
to chase and pounce
on her toys.

They know she loves to climb and stretch and scratch her claws. They give her special furniture to play on so she doesn't scratch the other furniture around the house.

They know she likes
sunny places to sleep...

...and soft, quiet places to hide.

No one plays with the unhappy cat.

She doesn't have toys to play with

or special furniture to climb and scratch.

Sometimes, she gets yelled at for just being a cat.

Every year, Happy visits
a veterinarian, a doctor
who takes care of animals.
Happy would rather stay
at home, but her family knows
she needs her shots
to stay healthy.

No one takes the unhappy cat

to the veterinarian,

even though she needs

to stay healthy too.

One day, the unhappy cat's family moves away.

Sadly, they leave her behind.

She meows, waiting for someone

to let her back into the house.

The unhappy cat is scared and alone.

A nice neighbor notices the empty house
and the unhappy cat on the porch.
She calls the animal shelter for help.

A kind lady from the animal shelter
rescues the unhappy cat.
She puts a blanket over the cage so
the unhappy cat is not scared.

"You're safe now," says the kind lady.
"I will take you to the animal shelter, the place
where we take care of other abandoned pets."

At the animal shelter, a veterinarian
examines the unhappy cat.
She looks into her ears and eyes
and gives her shots so she will be healthy.

This is the unhappy cat's first visit to a doctor.

She is not a happy cat yet.

"Your fur has not been brushed in a long time,"
says the kind lady. "Let's give you a bath."
She puts the unhappy cat into
a special bathing bag
to keep her calm.

This is the unhappy cat's first bath.

She still is not a happy cat.

"You must be hungry," says the kind lady.

She leaves the unhappy cat some food and a blanket

so she has a soft, quiet place to hide.

The unhappy cat is safe at the animal shelter.

Every day, the kind lady

visits the unhappy cat.

This is the unhappy cat's first friend.

One day, the kind lady gives her a collar and an ID tag with her new name on it. "We're naming you Happy because we want you to be a happy cat," she says. Happy purrs.

Happy waits at the animal shelter for many weeks. Most people adopt kittens, but older cats are wonderful too. Will she ever find a family to love?

One day, a nice family visits the animal shelter looking for a cat to adopt. The kind lady introduces them to Happy. She tells them that Happy is a friendly cat who loves to play with toys and hide in blankets. "Hey, that's our cat's name too!" says the girl.

The family spends most of the day getting to know Happy.
The little boy speaks softly to her. The little girl plays with her.

"We have to let her come to us," says mom.

Happy loves all the attention.

"Oh, I love her," says the little girl.

"Can we take her home?"
says the little boy.

"Yes, she's perfect,"
says dad. "Let's ask
if we can become
her new family."

The family asks if they can adopt Happy.

The kind lady says, "Yes, you know what cats need to be happy in their homes."

The kind lady prepares the adoption papers. She also tells them how to introduce Happy to the other cat already in their family.

"The best way for two new cats to meet each other is through a closed door," says the kind lady. "They need time to become good friends."

Now, in the very same town,
on the very same street,
in the very same house,
live two cats that share the love of
the same wonderful family.
They play. They sleep.
They help their family around the
house every day.

One cat has always been Happy.

Now the other cat can finally be called Happy too.

CPSIA information can be obtained
at www.ICGtesting.com
Printed in the USA
LVIC06n2219040814
397546LV00007B/36